THE DEMONS' MISTAKE

A Story from Chelm

By **Francine Prose**   Pictures by **Mark Podwal**

Greenwillow Books
An Imprint of HarperCollinsPublishers

For Johanna and Sarah
— F. P.

For Lucy
— M. P.

Gouache and colored pencils were used
for the full-color art.
The text type is Leawood Book.

The Demons' Mistake: A Story from Chelm
Text copyright © 2000 by Francine Prose
Illustrations copyright © 2000 by Mark Podwal
All rights reserved.
Printed in Singapore by Tien Wah Press.
www.harperchildrens.com

Library of Congress
Cataloging-in-Publication Data

Prose, Francine, (date)
The demons' mistake : a story from Chelm /
by Francine Prose ; illustrated by Mark Podwal.
    p.   cm.
"Greenwillow Books."
Summary: Demons from the town of Chelm
hide in a crate being shipped to New York
because they hope to practice their mischief
where streets are paved with gold and there
are parties every day.
ISBN 0-688-17565-1 (trade)
ISBN 0-688-17566-X (lib. bdg.)
[1. Chelm (Chelm, Poland)—Folklore.
2. Jews—Europe, Eastern—Folklore.
3. Folklore—Europe, Eastern.]
I. Podwal, Mark H., (date) ill. II. Title.
PZ8.1.P9348 Dg 2000
398.2'09438'4—dc21   [E]   99-056245

1 2 3 4 5 6 7 8 9 10 First Edition

The demons in the town of Chelm were going to a party.

There was nothing that the demons of Chelm liked better than a party. So many things can go wrong at a party, and they liked to make sure that everything went wrong. People go to parties to have fun. The way the demons had fun was to spoil the people's fun. Though demons are invisible and do not need to eat, one of their tricks was to gobble up all the food so that the guests wouldn't have any.

In most villages people took precautions against demons. They put salt in their pockets and wore red and white clothing. (Demons hate the colors red and white.) They drew circles around themselves for protection and made loud noises when they had to go out alone. (Demons are scared of loud noises.)

But in the town of Chelm the people were so simple, they kept their money and precious possessions outside their front doors, so thieves wouldn't break into their houses to steal them. A party in the town of Chelm was a big event for the demons.

Night was the demons' favorite time, and their favorite haunting places were the woods and fields and cemetery just outside Chelm and the dark, narrow lanes of the village itself. Demons need solitude, darkness, and quiet to do what they do best—scare people who are foolish enough to go out walking alone in the dark.

On the night of the party the demons gathered in the woods
or in the narrow lanes and waited for the guests on their way to
the home of Reb Pupkin and Mrs. Pupkin—the richest family in
Chelm. The Pupkins were giving the party for their son, Chaim,
who now lived in America and had come home for a visit.

As the horse-drawn cart carrying Schlomo the farmer and his wife and their ten children to the Pupkins' party hurried along the lonely road across a field, the demons herded a flock of sheep up into the sky. They flew in formation like a flock of geese. The frightened horses bolted, the cart turned over, and Schlomo, his wife, and children landed in a puddle of mud.

"I didn't know sheep could fly," said Schlomo's wife.

"The birds must have taught them," said Schlomo.

The farmer and his family went on to the party with their best clothes soaked and caked with mud.

The demons waited in the shadows the moon cast over Chelm Street until Grandma Lepinski passed by. Immediately they turned into a pack of alley cats walking on their hind legs, wearing hats and coats. They tipped their hats and said good morning, though it was night. Night or day, it was all the same to the demons. Grandma Lepinski was so frightened that when she got to the party, she had to sit down and take a pill.

Now the demons were ready to join the party. They flew through the gaps between the wooden beams of the Pupkins' house. Demons are invisible, and so of course no one saw them fly in. God created them on the very first Friday evening just before He rested for the Sabbath. He didn't have time to finish them. With their incomplete, winged bodies, the demons were much too terrifying to show themselves to humans.

Once in the house, the demons immediately set to work. They tangled people's hair, spilled drinks, made the milk go sour. And when the milk in Chelm went sour, someone had to run to the farmer and wait while the farmer milked the cow.

Another reason demons liked parties was that they loved gossip. In fact, they enjoyed it almost as much as they enjoyed quiet and the dark. It was said that when someone gossips, it is like opening the door and letting the demons in. When the demons heard Mrs. Lopetski announce that she saw Mrs. Bobetski secretly eating a big plate of bacon, the demons really went wild.

They rubbed against the guests and tore their clothes, sometimes in the most embarrassing places. They turned wine into vinegar, which the astonished guests could not help spitting out. Poor Reb Pupkin and Mrs. Pupkin. Only the children, who didn't care about their hair or their clothes or the wine, were having a good time.

Perched high in the rafters, the demons waited to see how much
mischief they could do, when all at once they heard Mrs. Pupkin say,
"Chaim, dear, tell our friends about America."

"My name is Charles now," said Chaim.

"That's odd," said Mrs. Pupkin. "I thought your name was Chaim."

"In America," said Chaim, "my name is Charles."

"Charles, dear," said Mrs. Pupkin, "tell our friends what New York
is like."

"First of all," said Chaim-Charles, "the streets really are paved with gold."

"With gold?" said Schlomo the farmer. "Then what do they use for jewelry?"

"Cobblestones," said Schlomo's wife.

"The streets are paved with gold," repeated Chaim-Charles. "And the buildings are made of silver and shine in the sun."

Chaim-Charles continued. "Everyone eats five meals a day, as much food as they want. Everyone drives a motor car. And there are parties every day, all day and all night."

Streets paved with gold! Parties every day! Right then and there the demons decided to go to America. But how in the world would they get there?

"We can just fly there," said a brave young demon called Zereda.

"It's very far," said the other demons. "Besides, what will stop us from flying off the edge of the earth?"

The demons considered taking the boat with Chaim-Charles. But suppose the boat had its own demons? Tough sailor-demons who might throw the Chelm demons overboard into the sea?

At last the demons had an idea. The Pupkins had packed a huge crate with the gifts that Chaim-Charles was to take back to America. Why not hide in the crate and get themselves *sent* to New York?

"Too slow!" said Zereda. "I'm flying. I'll meet you in New York."

In the middle of the night the demons sneaked into the shop of the carpenters where the crate waited to be shipped to America. Soon enough, but too late, the demons of Chelm discovered that Zereda had been right. It was a terrible idea! The crate was dark, and even though the demons love the dark, *this* darkness was hot and airless and crowded. The carpenter had built the crate so well that there were no gaps to fly out of.

And on the boat, the slow boat, that took the crate to America,

the demons learned something else: demons can get seasick.

What a frightful voyage! A storm came up, the boat pitched

and rocked.

But finally they stopped moving. They heard shouts and felt strong arms carrying the crate off the boat.

Now our troubles are almost over, the demons thought. But once more they were wrong. After all, the crate had come from Chelm, and no one had been smart enough to put an address on it. The crate went unclaimed and waited on the docks for a long period. After a few weeks it was taken to a warehouse, where it sat and sat and sat.

Fifty years went by. More than anything, demons hate being cooped up. As time passed, the demons got angrier and angrier, but no matter what they tried, they could not find a way to free themselves. Cobwebs covered the outside of the crate. Finally the warehouse grew so old and dilapidated that its owners decided to tear it down and auction off its contents.

The demons were all snoozing when suddenly it was daylight. Someone had yanked the lid off the crate.

The demons flew out into a strange new world. So much bustle and

commotion! It was true, what Chaim said. Everyone had a car! People

ate more than five meals a day! And though the streets were black,

not gold, the buildings *were* made of silver. Or anyway, that's how it

seemed to the demons of Chelm.

Bright moving pictures flashed on and off on the sides of buildings.

People walked down the street talking to little black objects, as if little

black objects could hear and understand.

But how were the demons supposed to practice their mischief in this new place? In New York there were always people around. There was no way for the demons to lurk in some deserted alley and scare someone foolish enough to be out and walking alone. There were no open fields to haunt—except for the parks, and people were very careful when they walked through the parks at night. There was always light from the streetlamps. There were no moon shadows and no darkness to hide in.

Once, the demons found some stairs leading into the ground, and they flew down the staircase hoping for quiet and darkness. Back in Chelm they used to hide deep down in old wells. They were overjoyed to find themselves in a shadowy tunnel—until suddenly a train roared through and the noise terrified them.

When the demons rubbed up against people in the city and tore holes in their coats, as they had loved to do in Chelm, most people didn't seem to mind. They just went into a shop on the corner and got the tears fixed. Others were glad to go shopping for a *new* coat.

In Chelm when people gossiped, it was said they were allowing the demons in, but in New York everyone gossiped all the time. There was gossip in the newspapers, in magazines, and even on those odd little boxes with moving pictures that everyone watched in their homes.

The demons still tangled people's hair, but in New York the victims just said they were having a "bad hair day" and went to a store, bought some lotion, and combed the tangles out.

The demons were in despair. What was the point of a whole new world if there was nothing in it for them to do?

One day on the street the demons found an invitation to a party. A party! Their spirits rose. Then they fell again. Why bother going to a party if there was no way to have fun there? If they made the milk go sour, the hosts would just go to the corner and get more. If they turned the wine to vinegar, there was always more wine to be had.

Finally the demons decided to take desperate measures. They would go to the party! And for the first time ever—the first time since they were created on the Friday evening of creation—they would show themselves to people, reveal themselves for all to see, and scare the party guests so badly they would all run home. Now *that* would be fun!

However, the night of the party just happened to be Halloween. At the party everyone was in costume. There were witches and devils and ghosts, and no one paid the demons the slightest bit of attention. No one even noticed that the demons had no shadows. In fact, everywhere the demons looked, they saw creatures that terrified *them*. It was the worst party the demons had ever been to!

Frightened and discouraged, the demons flew out into the street, where everyone was dressed in a scary costume. The people frightened the demons far more than the demons frightened them.

And then, in that crowd of masked and costumed revelers they saw a familiar face. It was Zereda.

"What took you so long?" he said.

How happy the demons were to see their lost friend! They told Zereda about their trip and about their problems in this new country.

"Don't you worry," said Zereda. "There are plenty of things for demons to do here. There is plenty of fun to be had. Come on. Just follow me."

Then Zereda showed the Chelm demons all the new ways they could make trouble in America—tricks the demons learned slowly.

But gradually they figured out how to get into people's computers and make awful things appear on the screen.

They changed the colors on traffic lights at busy corners, snarling

traffic for hours, so that many people were late getting to work.

And so the demons found that wherever they went,
there was always trouble to be made.

And they learned that they could travel wherever they wanted—
across the country, and all over the world.

So wherever you live, it might be a good idea to wear red and
white when you go out, and to carry a little salt in your pocket.